PUFFIN BOOKS

Sheltie and

Make

# Sheltie

## The little pony with the big heart

Sheltie is the lovable little Shetland pony with a big personality. He is cheeky, full of fun and has a heart of gold. His best friend and new owner is Emma, and together they have lots of exciting adventures.

Share Sheltie and Emma's adventures in

SHELTIE THE SHETLAND PONY
SHELTIE SAVES THE DAY
SHELTIE AND THE RUNAWAY
SHELTIE FINDS A FRIEND
SHELTIE TO THE RESCUE
SHELTIE IN DANGER
SHELTIE RIDES TO WIN
SHELTIE LEADS THE WAY

Peter Clover was born and went to school in London. He was a storyboard artist and illustrator before he began to put words to his pictures. He enjoys painting, travelling, cooking and keeping fit, and lives on the coast in Somerset.

*Also by Peter Clover in Puffin*

## The Sheltie series

1: SHELTIE THE SHETLAND PONY

2: SHELTIE SAVES THE DAY

3: SHELTIE AND THE RUNAWAY

4: SHELTIE FINDS A FRIEND

5: SHELTIE TO THE RESCUE

6: SHELTIE IN DANGER

7: SHELTIE RIDES TO WIN

9: SHELTIE LEADS THE WAY

# Sheltie and the
# Saddle Mystery

Peter Clover

PUFFIN BOOKS

*For Jenny, Peter and Daisy*

PUFFIN BOOKS

Published by the Penguin Group
Penguin Books Ltd, 27 Wrights Lane, London W8 5TZ, England
Penguin Putnam Inc., 375 Hudson Street, New York, New York 10014, USA
Penguin Books Australia Ltd, Ringwood, Victoria, Australia
Penguin Books Canada Ltd, 10 Alcorn Avenue, Toronto, Ontario, Canada M4V 3B2
Penguin Books (NZ) Ltd, 182–190 Wairau Road, Auckland 10, New Zealand

Penguin Books Ltd, Registered Offices: Harmondsworth, Middlesex, England

First published 1998
1 3 5 7 9 10 8 6 4 2

Copyright © Working Partners Ltd, 1998
All rights reserved

Created by Working Partners Ltd, London W12 7QY

The moral right of the author/illustrator has been asserted

Filmset in 14/20 Palatino

Made and printed in England by Clays Ltd, St Ives plc

Except in the United States of America, this book is sold subject to the condition that it shall
not, by way of trade or otherwise, be lent, re-sold, hired out, or otherwise
circulated without the publisher's prior consent in any form of binding or cover other than
that in which it is published and without a similar condition including this
condition being imposed on the subsequent purchaser

British Library Cataloguing in Publication Data
A CIP catalogue record for this book is available from the British Library

ISBN 0–140–38951–2

# Chapter One

Sheltie was all alone in his paddock. It was really quite early and Emma's Shetland pony had been awake for hours. It was too early for breakfast. And no matter how hard Sheltie stared at Emma's bedroom window from his favourite spot by the paddock gate, the bedroom curtains remained closed.

Every morning, Sheltie watched Emma's window and waited for her face to appear. But today she seemed to be taking ages. It had been raining almost non-stop for two days and Emma hadn't been able to take Sheltie out riding as often as usual.

The rain had stopped this morning, though, and the sun had broken through the ragged grey clouds. Everything smelt green and fresh. Sheltie felt frisky and alert. His nostrils twitched as he took in all the lovely country scents the rain had brought.

Sheltie had been cropping the grass for a good half-hour, but what he really wanted was his pony mix. The paddock was muddy, so Sheltie's feet and legs were covered with mud. He kept fidgeting and moving about, doing a funny little dance on the same spot. This only made matters worse and churned up the patch where he was standing even more.

Sheltie was getting bored. He tried a few loud whinnies and continued to watch Emma's window. But still nothing moved.

The little pony felt a sudden itch at his shoulder. He couldn't reach it with his teeth, so he decided to give himself a good scratch on one of the fence posts. There was a nice rough one, perfect for rubbing itches, at the far end of the paddock by the lane. Sheltie trotted over, squelching mud and grass beneath his little hooves. He found the rough post and leaned against it with all his weight, rubbing and scratching.

Sheltie closed his eyes. That felt much

better. And as the little pony rubbed his itchy shoulder, the post moved. Only a fraction, but enough to make Sheltie's ears prick up. He rubbed a little harder. Then he pushed some more until the post really wobbled in the soft earth.

He knew that if he pushed just a bit harder the post would lean right over and there would be a little gap for him to squeeze through.

So Sheltie pushed. And there it was. A narrow space just wide enough for a little Shetland pony.

Once Sheltie was out in the lane he tossed his head and swished his long tail. It almost touched the ground, and swept through the muddy puddles as he splish-sploshed up the lane to find his own breakfast.

4

Sheltie knew exactly where to go. Mr
Crock lived at the top end of the lane and
was always up bright and early. Mr
Crock was a keen gardener and grew
heaps of vegetables in his walled garden.
There was always a carrot or two going
whenever Sheltie visited Mr Crock.

Halfway along the lane, Sheltie
stopped. A small, grubby green van

splattered with mud was rumbling towards him. Someone else was obviously awake and about their business. Sheltie didn't recognize the van. He had never seen it before. And when the van stopped and two people got out, Sheltie didn't recognize them either. One man was older than the other, but they were both rough-looking.

'Look at that!' said the younger man. He was no more than a teenager. 'A baby horse.'

'It's not a horse, stupid,' said the other. 'It's a pony. A little Shetland pony.'

'What's it doing out on its own so early, Dad?' said the younger man. (His name was Jim.) 'Let's catch it.'

But Sheltie had no intention of being caught. As the men approached, Sheltie pawed the ground and let out two loud snorts.

'He looks fierce,' said Jim.

'Fierce! You're not scared of a little Shetland pony, are you?' said Jim's father.

Then, as Jim made a grab for Sheltie, Sheltie lurched forward and charged past them, bowling Jim out of the way. Jim sat down with a bump, right in the middle of a muddy puddle. He was really cross and yelled, but his father laughed as Sheltie trotted away down the lane to Mr Crock's vegetable garden.

Sheltie was a very clever pony and an expert at slipping bolts. He unlocked Mr Crock's gate and nudged it open. Then he plodded into the garden and whinnied for Mr Crock, hoping for a nice juicy carrot.

Mr Crock heard Sheltie and came out of his potting shed.

'Good morning, Sheltie. You're up bright and early.' The old man looked around for signs of Emma. He guessed that Sheltie had escaped and was taking himself for a morning stroll.

'Have you been naughty again, Sheltie?'

Sheltie blew a raspberry. He could be so cheeky sometimes.

'Have you come for a carrot?'

Sheltie looked appealingly at Mr Crock and raised his hoof.

'Come on, let's find you one. Then let's get you back home. Emma will be worried out of her wits when she finds you missing.'

# Chapter Two

Back at the cottage, Emma had just
woken up. It was the half-term holiday,
but she still got up nice and early.
Though not early enough today for
Sheltie. When Emma crossed to the
window and looked out into the paddock
she could see no sign of her little pony.

'Oh no!' said Emma.

She dressed really quickly and raced
down the stairs. Out in the garden Emma

called Sheltie's name. But Sheltie wasn't there to answer. She checked the fencing and soon found the gap where he had escaped.

Emma's heart missed a beat, but she knew where Sheltie would probably be. She began to hurry down the lane to Mr Crock's cottage. Halfway there she met Mr Crock walking Sheltie back the other way towards her.

'Sheltie!' called Emma. 'Where have you been?'

Sheltie blew a greeting and trotted towards her, his mane and tail bouncing. Mr Crock smiled. He didn't have to tell Emma what had happened. She knew exactly where Sheltie had been.

'I'm sorry if Sheltie has been a nuisance,' she said.

Mr Crock and Emma were friends. He said he didn't mind early-morning visits, but he was concerned that Sheltie had got out of his paddock.

'Up to his old tricks, the rascal.' He

smiled and gave Sheltie a good pat, then said goodbye.

'Come on, Sheltie. Let's get you back home. You've given Dad some extra work to do now, haven't you?'

Emma's dad had taken a few days holiday from work to do some odd jobs around the cottage. Now he had a paddock fence to mend as well.

Emma led Sheltie back to the cottage. She held on to Sheltie's mane and pretended she was a gypsy queen leading a wild pony in a fairy story.

She took Sheltie right up to the cottage. Joshua, Emma's little brother, came bouncing out all bright eyes and smiles.

'Hello, Sheltie,' he gurgled, and reached up to stroke the pony's soft velvety muzzle.

Sheltie stood very still and let Joshua stroke him. Mum looked out to see what was going on.

'Sheltie escaped,' said Emma. 'He pushed a fence post out and went to visit Mr Crock.'

'Oh dear,' said Mum. 'Looks like another job for Dad.'

She wasn't cross with Sheltie. He was such a lovable pony and it was part of his character to be naughty. Although sometimes it *was* a bother.

Emma fetched Sheltie's head collar and tethered him loosely to a ring in the stone wall of his field shelter. Then she gave him his pony mix to keep him occupied while she went inside for her own breakfast.

While Emma was busy shovelling

cornflakes into her mouth, Dad buttered
some toast and relaxed with his
newspaper.

After a few minutes he said, 'I don't
believe it!' He looked up from his
newspaper.

'What don't you believe?' asked Mum.

'This,' said Dad. 'Here in the paper. It says that there are rustlers in the area.'

'Rustlers! Here?' said Mum. 'Surely not. I thought rustlers only existed in the old Wild West.' She poured more tea.

'No. It appears that rustling still goes on, even in this part of the world. But in this case they seem to be stealing saddles rather than ponies. Especially new or expensive ones. According to the newspaper, three thefts have been reported in the last fortnight. One in Rilchester and two in Fenbury.'

'That's a bit too close to home,' said Mum.

'How awful,' said Emma. She felt really sorry for anyone who'd had their saddle stolen. 'Well, they'd better not try and steal Sheltie's, or I'll give them what for!'

'That's real fighting talk,' said Mum with a smile.

Emma spread a thick layer of strawberry jam on her toast. She was deep in thought.

'It would be so awful if someone stole Sheltie's saddle,' she said. 'I wouldn't be able to ride him properly. I'd have to go bareback.'

'There's no need to jump the gun, Emma,' said Dad, putting his newspaper down. 'I'm sure the thieves wouldn't be interested in Sheltie's old saddle anyway. Besides, it's so small. And there have been no reports of any thefts in Little Applewood.'

'But what about Sheltie's special

Sunday saddle? The one Marjorie Wallace gave him,' added Emma. 'That must be worth an awful lot of money.'

'Well, to be on the safe side, we'll just have to make sure the tack room is locked up every night, won't we? There, that's another job for you, Emma.'

Emma grinned and Dad went back to his newspaper.

He scanned the local adverts, then announced, 'This looks interesting.' There was an advertisement which read:

cash payıı

Wanted. Any scrap metal or jumble. Garage clearances. Odd jobs also undertaken for cash or part exchange. Call 013 240684

'I wonder,' said Dad. 'We've got a rusty old lawnmower that we don't use any more in the shed. And there's that old fridge and tin bath cluttering up the garage. The paddock fencing has quite a few posts that need mending. Perhaps we could clear out all our rubbish and get the repair work done in exchange.'

'There's my old sewing machine too,' added Mum. 'It would be a good exchange to have the paddock fencing fixed and get rid of all our clutter and jumble at the same time. Why don't you give the number a ring?'

'I think I'll do just that,' said Dad. 'Kill two birds with one stone.'

'We're not going to kill any birds, are we?' said Emma. She looked really concerned.

'Don't worry, Emma,' laughed Mum. 'Dad just means that we'll get two jobs done at the same time. It's only a saying.'

# Chapter Three

Dad telephoned the number in the advert straight after breakfast.

It was a mobile-phone number and a man answered it after four rings.

'Riley's Home Clearance and Repairs. How can I help you?'

Dad said that he had seen the ad, and explained the situation.

'The best thing to do is for me to come along and have a look. I'm sure we can

20

sort out something, sir. Some kind of arrangement.'

Dad gave the address of the cottage and Mr Riley said he would be there within the hour.

Then Dad went out to the paddock with Emma to release Sheltie and to make a temporary repair to the fence. He took a length of rope from the shed and tied the fence post back into position.

Sheltie looked on sheepishly. Although he didn't understand that he had done anything wrong, he seemed to know that he was responsible for whatever it was that Dad was doing.

Emma looked at the state of Sheltie's coat and decided to hose down his legs. They were caked with mud from the paddock. Sheltie stood still and allowed

Emma to hose and sponge him down.
Then she gave him a brush, and a
peppermint treat for being so good.

An hour passed quickly and both Emma
and Sheltie looked up when they heard
an exhaust backfiring out in the lane. A
battered green van pulled up and

stopped outside the cottage. It was the same green van that Sheltie had seen earlier that morning.

Sheltie made a rumbling noise in his throat, then gave a loud snort.

'What is it, boy?' said Emma. Sheltie trotted over to the side of the fence where the van was parked. Mr Riley and his son climbed out.

Dad was inside the cottage with Mum, sorting out the cupboard under the stairs. The old lawnmower was already propped up outside the shed along with the tin bath.

'It must be the fence people,' said Emma. She raced inside to fetch her parents.

It took less than ten minutes for Mr Riley and his son Jim to view the collection of articles on offer: the lawnmower, the bath, the sewing machine, the fridge and an odd assortment of junk that Mum and Dad didn't want any more.

'Mmm . . .' said Mr Riley. 'It would be worth our while to come to some arrangement. Let's take a look at the work you need doing.'

Dad led the two men over to the paddock fence and pointed out the dodgy posts. There were four in all that needed fixing. One needed replacing altogether, with some repair work to the rails.

Sheltie followed Mr Riley and Jim as they walked around the paddock testing the various posts. He recognized them from earlier that morning when he had

met them out in the lane. Sheltie
remembered how they had tried to grab
hold of him. He didn't like them one bit.
His ears went back and he kept tossing
his head.

The men ignored Sheltie, but Emma
thought there was something wrong. And

when Sheltie began to paw at the ground with his hoof, Emma looked puzzled.

'What's wrong, boy?' she said. She stroked his furry face. 'It's only two workmen come to mend your paddock fence. Don't be nervous.'

But Sheltie wasn't nervous. He just didn't like these two men and nobody else seemed to notice.

Finally, Mr Riley said, 'I think we can certainly do a deal. If we take away all your rubbish, we'll do your repair work in exchange, plus an extra ten pounds.'

Mum raised her eyebrows. Dad smiled. Ten pounds seemed a very fair price to get rid of all that junk and to have Sheltie's fence repaired.

They shook hands and Mr Riley arranged to come back the following day

26

with a bigger truck, to take everything away and start the work.

Everyone seemed happy except Sheltie.

The next day, Mr Riley and Jim returned with the truck. They loaded everything up, then set to work on the fence repairs. First they removed the old wobbly posts. Then they dug holes into which they were going to pour cement before refitting the posts. The paddock needed one brand-new post. The men were going to bring that along with the cement the next day.

They spent the rest of the afternoon hammering long nails into any loose rails around the paddock. By four o'clock they had finished that part of the work.

Meanwhile, Emma had to keep Sheltie

occupied and away from the gaps which the men had made in the fence when they'd dug the holes.

Part of the time, Sheltie had to be tethered in his field shelter. He didn't like that very much. But later on, when Emma's friend Sally and her pony, Minnow, came over, the two girls decided to take Sheltie and Minnow out for a long ride.

As they got ready to go, Mr Riley chatted to them while he packed up his tools. 'That looks like a very fine pony,' he said.

'I bet it costs a lot to keep a pony like that,' said Jim. 'What with feeding and the price of saddles and bridles and everything!'

Mr Riley smiled at Sally. 'I bet that

saddle cost your parents a fortune. It
looks like it's made of the finest leather.'

Sally felt pleased that they had noticed
Minnow's saddle. But Emma felt
uncomfortable. She suddenly
remembered the saddles that had been

reported stolen in the newspaper. She hurried Sally along.

When they were out and about riding through the countryside, Emma told Sally about the recent saddle thefts.

'That's awful,' said Sally. 'What a horrible thing to happen! Saddles are very special, aren't they, Emma? I've had mine ever since I've had Minnow. It was a special birthday present from my aunt. I'd hate to have it stolen. It's nicely worn in, and very comfortable for Minnow.'

'Well, let's hope the saddle thieves don't come round here,' said Emma. 'That's the last thing we need in Little Applewood!'

# Chapter Four

The next morning, Mr Riley and Jim
arrived bright and early with the new
fence post and the cement.

Emma had arranged to ride over to Fox
Hall Manor to meet Sally and Minnow
and spend the day practising their
jumping. Sally had a nice little course of
jumps set up in her back meadow. Emma
loved riding there. She felt like an
Olympic rider taking Sheltie over proper

jumps. Back in Sheltie's paddock there were only old bricks and planks of wood to practise with.

When Emma arrived at the big wrought-iron gates of the manor, she saw Police Constable Green's Range Rover parked outside. The gates were open and Emma rode Sheltie through and round to the back of the house, where Minnow's stable was.

She dismounted and led Sheltie to the loose box. A soft whickering came from Minnow's stable. The pony stuck his head over the door and nuzzled Emma's hand as she reached out to stroke him. Then he greeted Sheltie with a little snort. Sheltie whinnied and tossed his head in reply.

'Where's Sally?' asked Emma.

Minnow didn't look very happy. Emma could tell that something was wrong.

Then Emma heard the sound of footsteps on the cobbles. Mr Jones, Sally's father, appeared from round the corner. PC Green and Sally were with him. Sally's eyes were red and her face was blotchy. She had obviously been crying.

'Hello, Emma,' said Mr Jones. 'I'm glad you're here. Perhaps you can cheer Sally up.'

Fresh tears welled up in Sally's eyes.

'I'm afraid someone broke into the tack room during the night and stole Minnow's saddle,' said Sally's father.

'Oh no!' gasped Emma. 'Poor Sally. You must feel awful.' She put her arms around her friend and gave her a hug.

Unfortunately this only made Sally start crying again.

PC Green said he would try his best to find the thieves and the saddle. 'But I can't say that I hold out much hope,' he added. 'There have been several reports of saddle thefts in the district lately, and we're pretty sure the villains move the saddles to other parts of the country to sell them.'

Mr Jones was very angry about the stolen saddle, but he knew that PC Green would do everything he could to find it.

'Thank you for coming over, constable,' he said. 'Let me know as soon as you hear anything.'

'Make sure your tack room is safely locked up each night, Emma,' said the policeman. 'We don't want to encourage this sort of thing in Little Applewood.'

Emma promised, then went back to trying to cheer up her friend. She decided that the best way to help was to be as cheerful as possible herself. Minnow came up to the stable door again and blew gently down Sally's neck.

'Don't worry, Sally,' said Emma. 'You'll get Minnow's saddle back.' But she didn't feel quite as sure as she sounded.

'I'd lend you Sheltie's Sunday saddle, but it would be too small.'

Sally forced a smile. 'There must be something we can do, Emma. That saddle was special. It was Minnow's and now it's gone!' Another tear trickled down her cheek.

Then Emma had an idea. 'I know what we can do to get your saddle back,' she whispered. The two girls exchanged glances. Sally knew that some of Emma's ideas were impossible, but she was willing to listen.

'Let's go into the meadow and ride bareback for a while. Then I'll tell you my plan.' Emma wanted to be out of Mr Jones's earshot. She didn't want anyone to find out what she was up to.

Sally slipped on Minnow's bridle and led him down across the lawn. Emma led Sheltie to the meadow and then took off his saddle. Then the two girls rode their ponies bareback.

Sally cheered up a bit and began to enjoy herself. She had never ridden bareback before. It took some getting used to, but felt really comfortable.

Then Emma told Sally her plan.

'We'll set a trap for the robbers and catch them red-handed,' she said excitedly. 'I bet they won't have got rid of Minnow's saddle yet. They probably have to steal several to make it worth their while. So let's encourage them to steal Sheltie's!'

Sally looked down at Sheltie's saddle lying on the grass.

'I don't mean to sound rude,' said Sally. 'But Sheltie's saddle is rather small and very old, isn't it? Minnow's saddle was as good as new.'

'Not *that* saddle, silly,' said Emma. 'Sheltie's special Sunday saddle. It's beautiful.'

'Oh no. You can't do that, Emma! What if it really *does* get stolen? You can't lose

Sheltie's Sunday saddle. It's *so* special. It's got patterned work on it and must be very valuable. Besides, it was a present from Marjorie and Todd.' Sally sounded very anxious about Emma's plan.

'But it might work,' said Emma. 'And if it helps to get Minnow's saddle back and catch the thieves, then it will be worth it. Trust me, Sally. I have a feeling this will work.'

When Emma was determined, nothing could stop her.

'What we'll do is parade Sheltie's saddle around the village so that everyone can see it,' Emma explained. 'With any luck, the thieves will see it too and they'll come snooping round to Sheltie's tack room where we'll be waiting for them.'

Sheltie gave a loud snort and nodded his head.

'Yes, but –' Sally began.

'No buts,' said Emma. 'It's what we've got to do.' She was already hot on the trail of the saddle thieves. Emma was now the great detective and eager to put the first part of her plan into action.

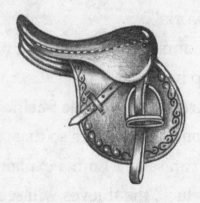

# Chapter Five

'Supposing the thieves *do* see Sheltie's Sunday saddle and *do* come snooping round Sheltie's tack room. What then?' asked Sally. 'How will we catch them? They're probably big men and we're only little girls.'

'Easy-peasy,' said Emma. 'We'll ask if you can sleep over at my place. Then after dark we'll sneak out and keep watch on the tack room. If we leave the tack-room door unlocked, the thieves will go inside. Then we strike!'

'Strike?' said Sally. It was all beginning to sound dangerous. 'Are you going to hit them, Emma?'

'No, silly,' Emma said with a laugh. 'We'll just lock them in, then get Dad to telephone the police.'

It sounded too easy. Sally wasn't so sure about the plan, but she didn't want to disappoint Emma, especially if Emma was willing to risk Sheltie's special Sunday saddle.

'OK. That's settled then,' said Emma. 'Let's get started straight away. We'll go home and I'll saddle up Sheltie and show him off around the village.'

Emma and Sally walked Sheltie home. They didn't tell anyone what they were

up to. Mr Jones was pleased to see that
Sally had brightened up. And when she
told him she was going over to Emma's
cottage, he didn't mind one bit.

Emma's mum and dad were busy in
the garden. Mr Riley and Jim were also
busy setting the fence posts in concrete.
But they did look up and stop working
when they saw Sheltie with his special
saddle.

'My, my, what a beautiful saddle,' said
Jim. 'It's much nicer than his old one,
isn't it?'

Sheltie blew a loud raspberry.

Emma grinned. 'It's Sheltie's special
Sunday saddle,' she chirped. 'It's worth a
fortune.'

'Well, you just make sure you take care
of it then,' said Mr Riley.

'I will,' said Emma. Then she winked at Sally and led Sheltie off down the lane to the village, to tempt any would-be robbers.

The rest of the morning, Emma and Sally paraded Sheltie all over Little Applewood. Sheltie really enjoyed

himself, but they didn't meet anyone that they didn't know or trust. They saw Mr Crock, Fred Berry, Marjorie Wallace and Mrs Pinkerton from the corner shop. They saw Charlie from the garage and lots of other people too. But no suspicious saddle thieves.

Sally came back with Emma to the cottage. When Mum heard about Minnow's saddle she was upset for Sally and invited her to stay for lunch. Dad telephoned the Manor to let Sally's parents know where she was.

In the afternoon the two girls talked through the second part of the plan. Emma asked if Sally could sleep over. Mum said it would be all right as long as Mr and Mrs Jones agreed. Emma was certain the answer would be yes, especially as Sally was so upset about Minnow's saddle.

Dad drove Sally home to fetch an overnight bag.

Emma's next brilliant idea was to ask Mum if she could put her tent up in the bedroom.

'We can use the sleeping bags and camp out inside,' said Emma brightly.

Mum thought it sounded like a fun idea and said she would help her. It was a metal-framed tent like an igloo and didn't need any guy ropes or pegs. It fitted perfectly in the space between Emma's bed and her wardrobe.

When Dad and Sally came back with Sally's things, the workmen were just finishing off in Sheltie's paddock. The posts were set and the concrete would

harden overnight. All that was left for
them to do was hammer the rails to the
new posts the next day and the job would
be complete. The gaps in the fence had
been covered with temporary boards to
stop Sheltie from escaping during the
night.

Sheltie was very interested in all the
work that had been going on and kept

looking at the new posts and tossing his head. And every time he saw Mr Riley and Jim he would snort loudly and his ears would go back. Emma was puzzled by Sheltie's strange behaviour. She couldn't understand why he didn't seem to like either Mr Riley or Jim. They were such nice, friendly people. But Sheltie thought differently.

# Chapter Six

That night, Emma and Sally camped out in the bedroom as planned. Joshua wanted to sit in the tent with Emma and Sally for a while before he went to bed. Emma read him a story by torchlight until he was sleepy and Mum carried him off to his own bedroom.

The two girls sat up late, chatting and discussing their plan. When Emma's mum and dad had gone to sleep, Emma and Sally were going to creep downstairs and out into the garden. Emma was going to unlock Sheltie's tack room and then they would hide and wait for the saddle thieves.

Emma felt really excited. Sally was more nervous than Emma, but thrilled at the idea of an adventure, even though it seemed dangerous.

Finally, Mum and Dad came upstairs to bed. Mum looked in on Emma and Sally. The two girls pretended to be asleep. But they lay quietly awake until they were certain that Emma's parents were sleeping themselves.

Then Emma and Sally got dressed and crept downstairs and out into the garden.

The moon shone brightly, so it didn't

seem very dark at all. Emma unlocked the tack-room door. Then they found a place to hide in the shadows behind the shrubbery, and watched.

Sheltie saw Emma and Sally from his paddock. He blew a snort and became frisky, stomping his feet and swishing his long tail.

'Shh, Sheltie!' whispered Emma. But Sheltie wouldn't quieten down until Emma went over and gave him a stroke and ruffled his mane.

Sheltie watched Emma as she went back into hiding and stood on guard, keeping a keen watchful eye on their hiding place.

Sheltie knew that something was going on.

'Let's hope that the robbers saw

Sheltie's saddle and fall into our trap,'
said Emma.

'I just hope I can stay awake,' said
Sally, yawning.

'I'll make sure you do!' said Emma. She
was wide awake and bursting with
excitement. She so much wanted to catch

the thieves and get Minnow's saddle
back.

The night was silent except for the
odd hoot from an owl in one of the trees.
A hedgehog snuffled around in the
bushes near by and for a moment Sally
was frightened. But Emma laughed and
then Sally felt silly. Her tiredness wore
off and she too became wide awake and
alert. But nothing seemed to happen.

Some grey ragged clouds passed
across the moon and the garden became
dark and filled with shadows. It was
spooky at first, but Emma knew that
Sheltie was not far away. If anyone came
snooping around, then Sheltie would
snort and give them a warning. Sheltie
stood with his fuzzy chin resting on the
top bar of the wooden gate. His ears

twitched at every noise, no matter how small.

More time passed and still nothing happened. Emma shone her torch briefly on to her watch. It was half-past one. The night ahead seemed endless.

The two girls kept awake by whispering their plan over and over. If the thieves came and went into the tack room, they would charge out together and push the door closed. A sliding bolt was fixed to the outside of the door, ready to be slipped across. They knew that they had the advantage of surprise. The thieves wouldn't be expecting anyone to leap out of the bushes and lock them in.

'But what if it all goes horribly wrong and they *do* manage to get away with

Sheltie's saddle?' worried Sally. 'What do we do then?'

Emma grinned. 'I've got a secret,' she said. 'Sheltie's saddle isn't in the tack room at all. I've taken it out and hidden it in the cupboard under our stairs.' Then she produced a big brass whistle. It was the old-fashioned kind that makes a lot of noise. 'If anything goes wrong I'll blow this. Want to give it a blow?'

Sally didn't. 'You'll wake your mum and dad up if you do. And then we'll be in *real* trouble!' But Sally did feel more confident knowing that Emma had the whistle. She was also glad that Sheltie's saddle was safe.

At half-past three the two girls decided that nothing was going to happen.

'It will be getting light in an hour or two,' said Emma. 'Looks like our plan hasn't worked.' Then she had another idea.

'We can make some posters advertising Sheltie's saddle for sale,' she explained. 'If we put them up all over Little Applewood then the thieves are bound to see them. And then they'll know for sure that there's a saddle worth stealing. I bet they won't be able to resist that!'

Emma went and said goodnight to Sheltie. She planted a big kiss on his nose and ruffled his forelock. Then Emma and Sally locked the tack-room door and crept back indoors and up the stairs to bed. Within minutes they were both fast asleep in the tent, exhausted.

*

The following morning Emma and Sally were still asleep when Joshua came bouncing into the room. He dived into the tent and the girls woke up with a start.

Emma sat up. 'What time is it?'

Sally rubbed her eyes and looked at her watch. 'It's just gone eight.'

'Come on, sleepyhead. We've got work to do!'

After feeding Sheltie and sitting down to their own breakfast, Emma and Sally set to work with felt pens and paper. They hid themselves away in the tent pretending to be playing explorers. They didn't want Emma's mum or dad to see what they were doing.

Joshua sat with them scribbling on a pad. He couldn't read what his sister was

writing, so it didn't matter that he was
there.

Emma and Sally made twenty posters.
Each one said:

Brand new leather
Saddle for sale.
Worth at least £200.
Bargain at £50.

Underneath they had written the address
of Emma's cottage.

# Chapter Seven

'Right,' said Emma. 'All we've got to do now is to stick these posters up all over Little Applewood. We'll take Sheltie with us to show off his saddle again. If this doesn't work, then nothing will.'

Sheltie looked up suddenly when he heard his name. He knew something was going on and pawed at the ground with his hoof.

Mum and Dad thought the two girls

were up to something, but didn't say a word. Sally didn't seem so unhappy any more, and they didn't want to spoil things.

Even when Emma asked if Sally could sleep over a second night and pitch the tent out in the garden, they didn't seem to mind.

Suddenly, Sheltie snatched one of the posters out of Emma's hand and raced across the paddock with it.

'Oh no!' said Emma. 'Quick, Sally, before anyone sees it.'

The two girls chased Sheltie in circles until he finally dropped the poster in exchange for a peppermint.

'Oh, Sheltie. You are so naughty!' Emma said, smiling.

Everything was set. Sally's parents had

said it was all right for her to stay over.
And Emma's mum had agreed to let
them move the tent out into the garden. It
was almost summer. There was no sign of
rain and the ground had already dried
out nicely. They could put up the tent

behind the shrubbery, where it wasn't far from the cottage, but couldn't be seen from the road.

That afternoon, Emma and Sally took Sheltie out and pinned up their posters all over Little Applewood. It would be impossible for anyone to miss them. All that remained was to be patient and wait until nightfall.

Emma crossed her fingers and held them up for Sally to see. Sheltie leaned forward to sniff them. Then he whinnied softly.

'Let's hope that the crooks take the bait and fall into our trap,' Emma said.

Sally smiled. Emma sounded like a television detective, hot on a case. She crossed her fingers too.

'Let's hope we can stay awake,' said Sally. Her mouth stretched open into a big yawn. 'We didn't get much sleep last night, did we?'

Sheltie was playing copycat. He lifted his head and opened his mouth, just like Sally.

Emma nudged Sally and made her jump. Emma laughed. 'That woke you up, didn't it?'

Sheltie snorted loudly and shook his mane as Sally grinned. 'You'll probably have to do that every five minutes,' she said.

Emma looked as though she was going to nudge Sally again. 'But not until tonight,' Sally added quickly. She didn't want to end up black and blue if it wasn't really necessary.

They went over to Horseshoe Pond for the rest of the afternoon. They took Sheltie with them and let him crop the grass as they sat beneath the sycamore tree watching the ducks on the water.

Sally hadn't brought Minnow with her and she missed him, but it was fun just sitting there and talking. Sheltie seemed to miss Minnow too and kept looking around for him and whickering softly.

It was almost teatime when they finally came back to the cottage. Mr Riley and Jim had finished the fence, been paid their wages and gone. Mum and Dad were both sitting at the kitchen table. In front of them, spread out across the table were at least ten of Emma's and Sally's posters.

When Emma saw their faces, she knew that she was in big trouble.

Mum didn't want to cause a fuss in front of Sally, but she asked about the posters all the same.

'What is the meaning of these, Emma?' she asked. 'Why on earth have you put Sheltie's saddle up for sale? We've had three callers at the cottage in the last half-hour. Surely you can't be thinking of selling Sheltie's special Sunday saddle.'

Emma had to think quickly. She hadn't expected Mum and Dad to find out about the posters. She hadn't even thought about the possibility of anyone actually turning up to buy Sheltie's Sunday saddle. The posters were meant to tempt the thieves. The plan had backfired!

'I'm sorry,' said Emma. 'It's just that

Sally was so sad when Minnow's saddle was stolen. I wanted to help and –'

'It's a nice thought, Emma,' Mum interrupted. 'But selling Sheltie's saddle to help Sally buy a new one isn't a good idea. And I don't think that Sally or her parents would really approve of it either.'

'After all, Emma, Sheltie's Sunday

saddle is very special and it *was* a present,' added Dad.

Sally turned bright red. She didn't know what to say, so she said, 'They're right, Emma. It's a very kind thought, but it's a silly idea offering Sheltie's saddle for sale. You can't do it.'

Emma gave Sally a look.

'I'm sorry,' Emma said. 'After tea I'll go out with Sheltie and take down the rest of the posters.' It was a lovely evening and Emma could cover the area easily within the hour. She looked at Sally again and raised her eyebrows.

'Phew! That was a close one, Sally,' whispered Emma as they went up to her room. 'Let's just hope the thieves have seen the posters too, before I take them down.'

'I felt awful,' said Sally.

'Me too,' agreed Emma.

After tea, Emma went off with Sheltie to gather up all the other posters just like she'd said she would. She was suddenly worried that Marjorie or Todd might have seen them too. What would they think? Emma hadn't thought of *that* possibility either.

Sally stayed at the cottage and played with Joshua until Emma returned. No more was said about the posters. Mum and Dad didn't want to embarrass Sally any further.

# Chapter Eight

Later that evening, when the sun had
disappeared behind the hills, Mum made
up a flask of hot chocolate and a little
parcel of crisps and biscuits for Emma
and Sally to take out to the tent.

'You might get hungry or want a drink
later,' said Mum. She sat in the tent with
the two girls for a little while after she
had put Joshua to bed. Later, Dad came
out too. It was cramped but cosy inside

the tent. Emma felt like an adventurous explorer and was looking forward to sleeping out under the stars.

It was a really warm evening and the sky was clear. Dad said he would leave the outside light on all night although it wasn't really that dark at all. The moon was full and bright. It shone in the dusky sky like a big silver ball. The grass looked silver too. The moonlight shone on Sheltie's mane, making him look like a ghost pony.

The little Shetland pony stood by the paddock gate watching the tent. His eyes were bright and alert. Sheltie could just make out a small corner of it poking out from behind the shrubbery next to the cottage. He knew that Emma was inside and wouldn't take his eyes off it.

All was quiet and peaceful in the
garden as Emma and Sally curled up in
their sleeping bags and waited. They each
had a torch and Emma had her big brass
whistle. Neither of the girls felt sleepy.
They were both wide awake and far too
excited.

'Isn't this fun?' said Sally. For a
moment she had forgotten why they were
really there. Then she suddenly
remembered and her tummy did a

somersault. 'I think I'll have one of those biscuits,' she said.

When they were certain that Mum and Dad were fast asleep, Emma and Sally crept out of the tent and unlocked the tack-room door. They left it slightly ajar. It was a perfect trap to catch a thief.

'Whatever happens, don't lose that whistle, Emma,' said Sally. She was beginning to feel rather nervous.

'I won't.' Emma had threaded a piece of string through it and hung it around her neck. She patted the whistle. 'They'll hear this at Scotland Yard!'

Sheltie had seen them out in the garden and blew several loud snorts. He was stamping his hoof by the gate and making quite a lot of noise.

'Shh!' whispered Emma. She put a

finger to her lips but she knew that Sheltie wouldn't quieten down until she went over to pet him.

It was lovely being out in the moonlight with Sheltie. Emma gave him a hug and he soon settled down and kept watch as Emma joined Sally back in the tent.

Sheltie knew something exciting was going on.

Emma and Sally decided to take turns looking out for the thief. If they peeped out of a flap at the tent's entrance, they could see the tack-room door quite clearly. But after a while Emma decided to watch from behind the large water-butt which was nearer. After all, if anyone did come, it would be a long way to run from the tent to the open door. And they might not be able to catch the thief in time. They could also see Sheltie quite clearly from there, and it was nice to know that he was watching too.

Sally took first watch. If anyone came she was to throw some gravel over the bushes on to the tent behind. But midnight passed and nothing happened. When it was Emma's turn, she crept out of the tent and over on tiptoe to the water-butt. She found Sally fast asleep.

'Sally!' snorted Emma. 'You're a fat lot of good!'

'Whaa?' said Sally sleepily. 'Oh! Sorry, Emma. I nodded off.'

Emma took up her position in hiding and Sally dragged herself off to the tent.

'And for goodness' sake, Sally. *Stay awake!*'

Sally grinned sheepishly.

Although it was the middle of the night, Emma could still see very well because the moon was shining so brightly. Every time Emma peeped over at Sheltie, he shook his long mane to let her know he could see her. As Emma crouched, waiting for the crooks to appear, her heart was thumping so loudly that she was worried someone would hear it.

Ten minutes later, Emma heard a noise.

Sheltie heard it too and raised his head suddenly.

A grubby green van drove up the lane and stopped at the garden gate. Behind the van was a small trailer. Emma gasped. It was the saddle thieves. Emma was sure of it. They had come. But why had they brought a trailer?

Suddenly, the answer dawned on Emma. It was only too clear. The trailer was just big enough for a small Shetland pony. They were going to steal Sheltie as well as the saddle!

Emma felt awful. If the thieves took Sheltie it would be all her fault.

Emma could hardly breathe. She threw

the handful of gravel over the bush on to the tent. But Sally was fast asleep inside and didn't stir.

Two figures got out of the van. Mr Riley and Jim! Emma could see them both as clear as day.

Emma's mouth dropped open. So *they* were the saddle thieves. She didn't want to believe it. They'd seemed such nice, friendly people.

Emma glanced around for a sign of Sally. But Sally didn't come.

'Sally!' hissed Emma. She didn't dare call any louder for fear of being heard. Should she blow her whistle and run indoors and fetch Dad? Emma didn't know what to do.

Suddenly her plan seemed very foolish indeed. She hadn't thought for one second that Sheltie might be in danger of being stolen.

At that moment, Jim took a pair of sturdy wire-cutters and a halter out of the van and went over to the paddock gate. He quickly snapped the padlock chain, pulled the safety pin and slipped the bolt across.

Sheltie pawed at the ground and snorted noisily as Jim pushed open the gate. Jim went into the paddock and Sheltie galloped away to the far side. But when Jim went after him, Sheltie ran at him and Jim had to jump out of the way. It wasn't going to be easy to catch Sheltie.

'Leave the pony for a moment, Jim,' said Mr Riley. 'Let's get the saddle first. Then we can both go after the Shetland.'

Emma breathed a sigh of relief. At least

Sheltie was safe for the moment. But for how long?

Jim came out of the paddock and closed the gate. Then he followed his father and tiptoed to the tack room. The door was ajar only metres from where Emma was hiding.

Mr Riley pulled the door open and

went inside. Jim followed. They didn't switch on the light and it was pitch dark inside. But Emma saw a torch flash and two shadows appeared framed in the doorway.

'You're sure there are pickings here, Dad?' Emma heard Jim say.

'That saddle must be here somewhere,' grunted Mr Riley. 'Look behind those sacks.'

It was now or never. With a tremendous surge of energy Emma flew out of her hiding place.

Sheltie saw Emma rush to the door and push it closed with all her strength. Then she shoved the bolt across.

'Here, what's going on?' shouted Jim, and thumped on the door.

Emma needed help – urgently. Quickly

Sheltie leaned over the gate and undid the catch with his mouth. Then he nudged the gate open and rushed up the garden to the tack room. Emma was so pleased to see him.

Inside the tack room Mr Riley and Jim banged on the door and threw themselves against it. They cursed and shouted, 'Let us out!'

The window was barred, but the door didn't look very strong. The bolt was going to give way at any moment. Sheltie saw what was happening and leaned all his weight against the door. No matter how hard Mr Riley and Jim pushed and shoved, they couldn't budge the little Shetland pony. Sheltie stood there, determined not to move an inch.

'Good boy, Sheltie,' Emma said,

smiling. Then she took the whistle and
gave it several long, noisy blasts.

'What's that?' Mr Riley's face appeared
at the window. 'It's that girl and her
flipping pony. They've got us locked in!'

'OK,' said Jim. His face appeared next
to Mr Riley's. 'You've had your fun,

Emma. It was a good game. Now let us out and we can go home.'

Sheltie blew a warning snort and Emma wouldn't let them out. Instead, she blew the whistle again, and this time Sally came racing out of the tent. At the same moment the upstairs window flew open and Dad peered out.

'Come quickly, Dad,' shouted Emma. 'We've trapped them! Sheltie and I have caught the saddle thieves!'

To Emma's relief, Dad was downstairs and outside in seconds, with Mum running along behind him. It was all very well playing detective, but Emma suddenly realized how frightening and dangerous it was. If it wasn't for Sheltie standing guard, Emma was certain that the two men would burst through the door at any minute. And then what? Emma quickly told Mum and Dad what had happened.

'Emma, go back into the cottage with Sally and Mum, now! And telephone the police.' Dad sounded really cross.

He waited with Sheltie for the police to arrive.

Emma and Sally watched with Mum through the kitchen window.

Outside, Mr Riley and Jim were still trying to escape, but Sheltie was a very strong little pony and wouldn't budge.

Two policemen arrived in a Range Rover. It was PC Green and PC McDonald. Seeing them, Sheltie moved away from the door.

Mr Riley and Jim had given up any hope of getting away now, but made up a story that they were looking for some tools they thought they had left behind.

'Well, let's just take a look then, shall we?' said PC Green as he snapped handcuffs on to the two villains.

He flicked on the light. Inside, the tack room was empty. There was no saddle and no tools either. Just Sheltie's bridle and grooming brushes, along with a store of pony mix in sacks.

When PC McDonald looked inside Mr Riley's van, he found Minnow's stolen saddle. Mr Riley couldn't explain *that* away. The pair of them had been caught red-handed.

'You seem to have caught two very nasty rats in your trap,' said PC Green. He smiled at Emma and Sally and told them how foolish they had been to try and catch the thieves on their own without telling anyone. 'You should leave this sort of thing to the police!'

Dad wasn't too happy to hear about Emma's plan either. He was quite angry. 'You should have told us what you were up to, Emma. These two could have been very dangerous and you might have been hurt.'

Still, there was no harm done, and

Mum and Dad were very glad to have Emma safe and sound.

'We couldn't just sit back and let them steal people's saddles,' said Emma. 'They had to be caught.'

Emma fancied the idea of joining the police force herself when she grew up. She explained this to PC Green. 'And don't you think Sheltie would make a smashing police pony?' she added. 'He may be small, but he's very brave and clever. He's got a nose for trouble.'

'I can believe that,' said PC Green, and Sheltie gave him a playful nudge as he led the two culprits away.

'I'm afraid we'll need Minnow's saddle for evidence,' said PC McDonald. 'But we can let you have it back in a day or two, Sally.'

Sally hoped she wasn't going to get into too much trouble when her parents found out.

The next morning, Sally's father came over to the cottage. He sat down with Emma, Sally and Emma's parents, and gave the two girls a real telling-off.

But nobody stayed cross with them for long. After all, they had been clever to catch the thieves and promised that they would never do anything like that again. As a punishment Emma and Sally were to go without television for a whole week.

Later that morning, after Mr Jones had taken Sally home, Emma wrote a letter to Sally's parents to say that she was sorry for getting Sally into trouble. She took it to the Manor herself.

*

Sally got Minnow's saddle back after a few days, and the two girls went riding over to Barrow Hill.

Sally felt very happy to be back in Minnow's saddle. She couldn't really explain to Emma how awful it was to have had it stolen. But Emma understood. She remembered how terrible she'd felt when she'd thought that Mr Riley and Jim were going to take Sheltie. That would have broken Emma's heart. She leaned forward on to Sheltie's neck and gave him a hug and a kiss.

'And to think', said Emma, 'that I put Sheltie in danger. I'll never do that again – ever!'

'You know,' she said, 'we can see for miles up here. All over Little Applewood.

This is the perfect spot for ponies on patrol. I know we're not old enough to join the police force yet, but we could keep an eye open for any trouble, couldn't we?'

'*Emma!*' said Sally. 'We promised.'

'We won't *do* anything. We'll just keep our eyes open, that's all. I'll be the chief

detective and you can be my trusty assistant.' Emma's grin spread wide across her face.

'I'll be second in command or I won't do it at all,' said Sally playfully, with a yawn. Emma reached over and poked Sally in the ribs.

'Same thing, isn't it?' she laughed.

Sheltie joined in with a funny snort that sounded a little like a laugh.

'Come on, sleepyhead, I'll race you to the stream,' said Emma.

Then she squeezed Sheltie with her knees and galloped away down the slope.